An AudioCraft Publishing, Inc. book

No part of this publication may be reproduced in whole or in part, or stored in a retrieval system, or transmitted in any form or by any means, electronic, mechanic, photocopying, recording, or otherwise, without written permission from the publisher. For information regarding permission, write to: AudioCraft Publishing, Inc., PO Box 281, Topinabee Island, MI 49791

Freddie Fernortner, Fearless First Grader
#10: The Pond Monster
ISBN-13 digit: 978-1-893699-72-4

Illustrations by Cartoon Studios, Battle Creek, Michigan

Visit www.americanchillers.com

Printed in the United States of America

Dickinson Press Inc., Grand Rapids, MI - USA Job#36283

THE
POND
MONSTER

VISIT CHILLERMANIA!

WORLD HEADQUARTERS FOR BOOKS BY JOHNATHAN RAND!

CHILLERMANIA!

**I-75 Exit 313
then south
1 mile!**

Visit the HOME for books by Johnathan Rand! Featuring books, hats, shirts, bookmarks and other cool stuff not available anywhere else in the world! Plus, watch the American Chillers website for news of special events and signings at **CHILLERMANIA!** with author Johnathan Rand! Located in northern lower Michigan, on I-75! Take exit 313 . . . then south 1 mile! For more info, call (231) 238-0338. And be afraid! Be veeeery afraaaaaaiiiid . . . .

1

This is the story of how Freddie Fernortner, fearless first grader, discovered a giant monster living in a nearby pond. It's an exciting story, but it's also a bit scary, so you might not want to read it under the covers with a flashlight.

"This is going to be fun," Freddie said to his friends, Chipper and Darla. The three were gathered on Freddie's front porch.

"I've never seen a real, live monster before," Darla said. "I'll bet he's really big."

"I don't think there is a pond monster," Chipper said. "I think your brother is only trying to fool you."

You see, that's how the three first graders first learned about the pond monster. Darla's older brother had told her all about the creature, and the three friends decided to look for it. They would go to the pond across the street and see for themselves.

"Do you want to help find the pond monster, Mr. Chewy?" Freddie asked. Mr. Chewy was Freddie's cat. Freddie named him 'Mr. Chewy' because he liked to chew gum and blow bubbles.

Mr. Chewy bobbed his head.

"All right," Freddie said. "Let's go find that monster!"

The pond wasn't very far away, and it only took them a minute to reach it. It was a small pond, too, with long cattails growing in the water near the shore. Lily pads also grew in the water, and there was a wooden dock, painted white, stretching out over the surface.

When they reached the edge of the pond, the three first graders stopped and looked around.

On the far side of the pond, a red-winged blackbird sat on the stem of a cattail. Several frogs croaked. A few bugs buzzed.

But they didn't see any sign of the pond monster.

"My brother says the pond monster could be anywhere," Darla said. "He can live in the water and in the woods."

"Let's walk out onto the dock," Freddie said, and he led the way. Mr. Chewy followed, chewing his gum and blowing bubbles.

Darla looked down. "The water sure is dark," she said. "I can't even see the bottom."

It was true. When they looked down into the pond, the water was very, very dark.

They stopped at the end of the dock. On the other side of the pond, the red-winged blackbird took flight and vanished over the treetops. Frogs continued to croak.

Still, there was no sign of the pond monster.

"See?" Chipper said. "There's no such thing as a pond monster."

But at that very moment, something horrifying happened. Beneath the dock, a giant shadow appeared in the water, right under the three first graders!

The pond monster!

2

When Freddie, Chipper, and Darla saw the big shadow in the water beneath them, they screamed. Darla raced down the dock until she reached the shore. She covered her face with her hands.

"Run, you guys!" she shrieked.

Freddie and Chipper, however, stayed on the dock. They were frozen in terror, and couldn't move.

Suddenly, the pond monster broke the surface, and Freddie and Chipper let out sighs of relief. It wasn't a monster, after all! It was just a big snapping turtle!

"You sure scared us, Mr. Turtle," Freddie said.

The turtle just glared at them, like he was looking at two creatures from outer space. Then, his head went below the surface and he vanished into the dark water.

"I thought that was the pond monster!" Darla said. "I thought he was going to gobble us up!"

"It was just a snapping turtle," Freddie said. He walked along the dock and back to shore. Chipper followed.

"Let's walk around the pond to see if we can find it," said Freddie.

Chipper nodded. "Good idea," he said.

The three first graders walked along the water's edge, searching the pond and the weeds that grew all around. Mr. Chewy wove around the bushes and through the tall, wispy grass.

"Did your brother say how big the pond monster is?" Freddie asked Darla.

"He said that he's huge, and he's very scary," Darla replied, spreading her arms wide. "He lives in the water, but he comes out onto the shore, too. Just like a turtle or a frog. My brother said that the pond monster could eat us up in one gulp."

"Maybe he only comes out at night," Freddie said.

"Maybe there's no such thing as the pond monster," said Chipper.

"Well," said Freddie, "if he's here, we'll find him."

They waded through the tall weeds and followed the shore to the other side of the pond. Mr. Chewy was last, chewing his gum and blowing bubbles. A frog that had been hiding in the tall grass near the pond leapt from a lily pad, splashed into the water, and vanished.

"I wonder if there are any bullfrogs here," Chipper said. "I've always wanted to catch one. I've seen bullfrogs almost as big as Mr. Chewy!"

They continued searching, looking in the weeds and dark water for any sign of the mysterious pond monster. They looked all around, but saw no sign of the creature.

"He's not over on this side of the pond, either," Chipper said.

"I'll bet he's hiding under water," Darla said. "He's waiting for one of us to fall in."

The three first graders stood at the water's edge, staring into the murky pond, looking for the pond monster . . . and they had no idea that something was coming up behind them in the woods!

3

There was a very loud snap—a breaking branch—behind them. Freddie, Chipper, and Darla spun. They were sure it was the pond monster coming after them.

But it wasn't. It was just a man. He was wearing jeans, a red shirt, and a blue baseball hat. He was carrying a fishing tackle box in one hand and a fishing pole and a net in the other. He was smiling, and he looked friendly.

"Hello," he said as he walked toward them.

"Hi," said the three first graders.

"A great day for fishing, don't you think?" the man said as he looked up into the sky.

"Yeah," said Freddie. "Are there fish in the pond?"

The man nodded. "Yes, there are," he said. "Hopefully, I'll catch some today."

"I hope you don't catch the pond monster," Darla said.

"The pond monster?" the man asked.

Darla nodded. "My brother told me all about him," she said. "He's big, and he's ugly, and he lives somewhere around here."

"Have you ever seen him?" Chipper asked the man.

The man shook his head. "No, I don't

24

think I have," he said. "He sounds scary."

"He is," Darla said. "We're looking for him right now."

"Well, if I see him," the man said, "I'll let you know."

Then, the man strode to the other side of the pond where he walked out onto the dock. He placed the tackle box and net at his feet, drew his fishing pole back, and cast his line into the water.

"I say we go home for lunch," Freddie said.

"Good idea," said Chipper. "I'm hungry. And, like I said: I don't think there is any such thing as a pond monster."

"I'll bet there is," Darla said. "He's just hiding."

"Maybe we'll come back and look for him tomorrow," said Freddie.

The three first graders and Mr. Chewy walked around the pond.

"Good luck," Freddie shouted to the fisherman on the dock.

"The man smiled and waved.

"What else can we do today?" Chipper asked.

Freddie began to speak. "We can—"

Suddenly, he was interrupted by the frantic shouts of the fisherman on the dock. The three first graders turned to see the man grasping his fishing pole. The rod was bent in a sharp arc.

"I've got one!" the fisherman shouted. *"I've got one!"*

Freddie, Chipper, Darla, and Mr. Chewy turned around and raced out onto the dock. They were anxious to see the fish the man was reeling in.

Then, the fishing pole suddenly went straight.

"Oh, no," the man said, shaking his head. "He got away."

"What kind of fish was it?" Chipper asked.

The fisherman shook his head. "I'm not sure what it was," he replied, "but I'll tell you one thing: he was a real monster!"

The three first graders gasped.

It was true! There really was a monster living in the pond!

4

As Freddie, Chipper, Darla, and Mr. Chewy walked home, they talked about the pond monster.

"My brother was right!" Darla said.

"Yeah," Freddie replied. "That guy almost caught the pond monster! He's so big, he broke the fishing line!"

"I didn't think there really *was* a pond monster," Chipper said.

"We should call the police," Darla said. "The pond monster might be dangerous."

"He might be," Chipper said. "But if the three of us stay together, we'll be safe."

Chipper and Darla went to their houses for lunch, and Mr. Chewy followed Freddie home. His mother had made a peanut butter and jelly sandwich for him. While he ate at the table, he told her about the pond monster.

"The fisherman almost caught him, Mom!" he said.

"What kind of monster is it?" his mother asked.

Freddie shrugged. "We don't know. But we're going to go back tomorrow to find him."

That night, Freddie had a very strange dream. He dreamed that he was walking near the edge of the pond when, suddenly, the pond monster emerged from the dark water. In his dream, the monster had black scales and a long nose. His eyes were red and glowed like fire, and his teeth were long and sharp. It was such a scary dream that Freddie awoke and sat up in bed.

Mr. Chewy was curled up on the floor.

"Whew," Freddie whispered. Mr. Chewy woke up and looked at him. "It was just a dream, Mr. Chewy," he said quietly.

He looked around his room. Some of the shadows were long and tall; others were short and wide. He lay back on his bed.

Tomorrow, he thought as he closed his eyes, *tomorrow, we're going to find the real pond monster, and we'll see what he* really *looks like. I hope he doesn't look like the creature in my dream!*

Oh, Freddie would get his wish. The very next day, he, Chipper, Darla, and Mr.

Chewy would discover the truth about the pond monster . . . but it would be one of the most frightening days of their lives.

5

Freddie awoke the next morning to the pattering of rain on the roof. He crawled out of bed, walked to his bedroom window, and stared outside.

The sky was dark and gray. A light drizzle was falling, and the green grass was shiny and wet. Droplets of water dripped from the trees and the lamp post. A car went by, its windshield wipers batting back and forth.

Across the street, Mr. and Mrs. Beaker's big dog, Booper, was sniffing the bushes and wagging his tail. The dog was soaked from the rain, but it didn't seem to bother him at all. Booper was a nice dog, and Freddie often saw him around the neighborhood. In fact, when Freddie had his dog walking service, he walked Booper around the block.

"I guess we won't be going to the pond today, Mr. Chewy," he said.

Mr. Chewy yawned and stretched, and Freddie left his bedroom and walked into the kitchen. His mother and father were at the table, sipping coffee and reading a newspaper. The scent of bacon and eggs filled the room.

"Good morning, Freddie," his dad said cheerily.

"Hi, Dad. Hi, Mom," Freddie said as he yawned and took his place at the table.

"Would you like some scrambled eggs?" his mother asked.

Freddie nodded. "And orange juice, too," he said. "Thanks."

His mother got up to fix his breakfast.

"I had a crazy dream last night," Freddie said. "It was so scary that it woke me up."

Freddie's father placed the newspaper on the table. "What was it about?" he asked.

"The pond monster," Freddie replied. "I had a dream about him. He was ugly with scales all over, and he had glowing red eyes and long fangs."

"That *does* sound very scary," Freddie's mother said as she placed a plate of scrambled eggs and bacon on the table. Freddie picked up his fork.

"It *was* scary," said Freddie as he nodded his head. "But it was just a dream. Chipper,

Darla and I are going to try to find the *real* pond monster today, if it stops raining."

As luck would have it, the rain ended later that morning. Darla and Chipper met Freddie on his front porch, where they made plans.

"Do you really think we'll find him?" Darla asked.

Freddie shrugged. "I don't know," he said. "But we'll have to be careful when we get to the pond."

"I don't want to be eaten by a pond monster," Darla said.

"Don't worry," said Chipper. "We'll be careful."

And so, the three first graders crossed the street and returned to the pond. Above, the sky was gray and dark. A light wind stirred the trees. The cattails that grew around the pond swayed gently, and ripples formed on the surface of the pond.

Freddie, Chipper, Darla, and Mr. Chewy approached the water carefully, on the lookout for the pond monster. When they reached the edge of the water, Freddie looked down.

His eyes flew open wide, and he quickly pointed to the muddy ground. There, in the soft earth, were strange footprints in the mud.

Monster tracks!

6

The three horrified first graders looked at the tracks. They were very large.

"My gosh," Chipper said as he knelt down. "These tracks are almost as big as my feet! The monster must be gigantic!"

"As big as a house!" Darla said.

Freddie knelt down for a closer look. "Yep," he said with a nod. "These look like monster tracks. He could be watching us at this very moment."

They looked around nervously. Mr. Chewy sat nearby, chewing his gum. He, too, was nervous.

"I'll bet he's in the pond, right now," Freddie said. "I'll bet he's hungry, too."

"Hey," Chipper said, "that gives me an idea."

"What's that?" Freddie asked.

"Let's see if we can trick him," Chipper replied. "Let's see if we can feed him something. We can toss something into the water and see if the monster eats it."

"That's a great idea!" Freddie said. "If we throw something in that floats, the monster might come to the surface to eat it. If he does, then we'll get to see what he looks like!"

"What do pond monsters eat?" Darla

asked.

"Probably anything," Chipper replied.

"I know," Freddie said. "Let's try a small stuffed animal. I have a bunch that I won at the fair last year. We can toss one into the lake and see if the monster eats it. You guys wait here, and I'll go get one."

Freddie raced home and returned, carrying a small stuffed bunny rabbit about the size of a softball. It was blue with a white ribbon around its neck.

"Do you think it will work?" Chipper asked.

Freddie shrugged. "I don't know," he replied.

"It will probably make the pond monster mad," Darla said. "I'll bet the bunny will taste yucky, and he'll spit it out."

"There's only one way to know for sure," Freddie said. Carrying the blue bunny, he strode out onto the dock, while Chipper, Darla, and Mr. Chewy waited on the shore. Then, Freddie drew his arm back and threw the stuffed animal into the lake.

The bunny hit the water with a soft splash, creating a ring of ripples.

Nothing happened.

The ring of ripples grew wider.

Still, nothing happened.

Then, there was a loud splash, and an explosion of water near the middle of the pond—right where Freddie had thrown the blue bunny!

The pond monster had eaten the stuffed animal!

7

Freddie, standing on the dock, stared. He'd tossed the stuffed bunny into the lake, and now it was gone. The pond monster had attacked and eaten it!

He spun and sprinted along the dock until he reached the shore where Chipper, Darla, and Mr. Chewy were waiting.

"Did you see that?!?!" Freddie asked.

"We did!" Chipper said. "The pond

monster ate your stuffed bunny!"

"I saw the monster's head!" Freddie said. "He has a long, pointed nose and big eyes, almost like my dream!"

"This is scary," Darla said. "What if he tries to gobble us up, just like the stuffed bunny?"

The three first graders thought about this. They didn't want to be gobbled up by the pond monster.

"Let's tell my mom," Freddie suggested. "She'll know what to do."

"But Freddie," Chipper said. "What if your mom doesn't believe you?"

"Yeah," said Darla. "She didn't believe you when you told her about the dust bunnies from outer space."

Darla was right. When Freddie, Chipper, Darla, and Mr. Chewy had been attacked by strange alien creatures that lived under his bed, his mother hadn't believed him.

"Maybe she will, this time," Freddie said.

A short time later, the three first graders stood in the kitchen at Freddie's house, explaining to his mother what they had discovered in the pond.

"You have to believe us, Mom," Freddie pleaded. "There's a monster living in the pond. Even the fisherman said so. It broke his line yesterday."

"And it gobbled up a stuffed bunny rabbit," Darla said. "We saw it happen!"

"Whatever you saw," Freddie's mother said, "I'm sure it wasn't a monster. There is no such thing as pond monsters."

They tried and tried, but Freddie's mother wouldn't believe them. Finally, they gave up.

Later, they sat on Freddie's porch, wondering what to do. Mr. Chewy sat on the sidewalk, chewing his gum and watching a bumblebee climb on a dandelion.

"I say we go back to the pond one more time," Chipper said. "Let's try to get a better look at the monster."

"Yeah," Freddie agreed. "Maybe, if we wait long enough, we'll even see the monster coming out of the water."

"Not me," Darla said, shaking her head.

"We'll be all right, Darla," said Freddie. "Nothing will happen to us."

"I don't know," Darla said warily.

"Oh, come on, Darla," Chipper said. "We'll be fine."

Finally, Freddie and Chipper were able to convince Darla to join them. The three friends hiked back to the pond with Mr.

Chewy scampering at their ankles.

And it was there, at the water's edge, where the three first graders made a horrifying discovery.

At the end of the dock, a tackle box sat. Next to it was a fishing pole and a net. In the water, near the middle of the pond, a blue baseball hat floated . . . but the man they had met the day before was nowhere to be found.

The pond monster had gobbled up the fisherman!

8

"*Oh, no,*" Freddie whispered. *"The pond monster ate the fisherman!"*

"And look!" said Darla. She pointed to the muddy ground at her feet. "There are monster tracks all over the place!"

Sure enough, there were more of the large, strange footprints in the mud . . . tracks they were sure had been left behind by the pond monster.

"What should we do?" Chipper asked.

"I don't know," Freddie said.

The three first graders could only stare at the hat, floating in the middle of the pond.

"That poor fisherman," Darla said.

"This is serious," said Chipper. "If the pond monster ate the fisherman, he could eat us, too!"

Then, there was a noise from the woods.

"It's the pond monster!" hissed Darla. *"I just know it is!"*

The three first graders huddled together, staring across the pond and into the woods on the other side. Mr. Chewy hid behind Freddie's leg.

They needn't have worried. It was just the fisherman. When he saw Freddie, Chipper, and Darla, he waved. He walked around the pond and stopped at the dock.

"Hello," he said.

"Hi," Freddie said. He pointed to the man's hat in the water. "We thought you were eaten by the pond monster!"

The fisherman turned. "Oh," he said. "The wind must have blown my hat off the dock. I left it sitting on my tackle box while I went home to get a bite to eat."

After he spoke, the fisherman walked out onto the dock.

"I wonder how he's going to get his hat," Darla said.

"He's not going to swim for it," Chipper said. "Not while there's a monster in the pond."

The three friends watched as the man picked up his fishing pole and cast the lure over the pond. The lure went up into the air, and landed right on top of the hat! The hook

54

caught on the hat, and the man began reeling it in.

"He's a good fisherman," Freddie said.

"I'm just glad he wasn't gobbled up by the pond monster," Darla said.

While they watched, the fisherman continued reeling in his hat. When it was near the dock, he knelt down, pulled it from the pond, and removed the fishhook. Then, he shook the water from the hat and put it on his head.

"Good as new!" he said with a smile. Then, he cast his line out again, in hopes of catching a fish.

"I have an idea," Freddie said. "Let's follow the monster tracks around the pond. They might lead us to the creature."

"I hope he doesn't gobble us up like he gobbled up the stuffed bunny," Darla said.

They began following the tracks in the soft earth, weaving around tall bushes and grass. The monster tracks were big, and very easy to follow.

Suddenly, Chipper spotted something, and he stopped.

"*Oh, my gosh!*" he exclaimed, pointing down into a clump of grass. "*Look at that!*"

Was it the pond monster? Turn the page to find out!

9

Freddie and Darla looked where Chipper was pointing. At first, they didn't see anything.

"What?" Darla asked. "What do you see, Chipper?" She took a step backward, because she thought it might be the pond monster.

"It's a bullfrog!" Chipper said. "And he's *huge!*"

Still, Freddie and Darla couldn't see the creature, because the bullfrog was the same color of green as the blades of grass and the bushes. He was very well hidden in the weeds.

"I see him!" Freddie suddenly said.

"Me, too!" Darla said.

"I'm going to catch him," Chipper said. "I'm an expert at catching frogs, but I've never caught a bullfrog before! You guys stay where you are and don't move, or you'll scare him away!"

Freddie and Darla did as Chipper asked. Even Mr. Chewy remained motionless, so he wouldn't scare the big bullfrog.

Slowly, Chipper took a step closer to the bullfrog. Cautiously, he raised his right hand. Still moving slowly, he took another step.

"I hope you catch him," Darla whispered.

"I will," Chipper said. "You just watch me."

Chipper continued to move slowly, being careful not to scare the bullfrog. He knelt closer, ready to move fast, to reach out quickly with his right hand and capture the creature.

"Here goes," he said softly.

Suddenly, his right hand shot out . . . but the frog was faster. At the same time Chipper moved, the bullfrog made a leap with his powerful hind legs. He landed in the water a few feet away and floated, looking back at Chipper with beady, black eyes.

"Rats," Darla said.

"Oh, I'm going to catch him," Chipper said. "I'm not giving up yet."

And with that, Chipper raised one leg and stepped into the pond! The water went up over his sneaker!

"What are you doing?!?!" Freddie asked.

"Your shoe is soaked!"

"It'll dry," Chipper said, still watching the bullfrog. "Catching this guy is a lot more important than a wet shoe."

"You're mom is going to be really mad at you," Darla said. "Your shoe and sock is all wet."

Chipper said nothing. Instead, he leaned closer to the water, intent on capturing the bright green bullfrog floating in the pond.

But, when he tried to catch the bullfrog once again, he was still too slow. The creature quickly turned and dove beneath the surface, vanishing in the murky water.

"Bummer," Freddie said. "I was really hoping you'd catch him."

"Me, too," Chipper said. He sounded disappointed. He turned and was about to pull his foot from the water . . . but it was at that very moment that the pond monster attacked, grabbing his sneaker! The creature was pulling Chipper into the pond!

10

"Aaaahh!" Chipper screamed. "It's got me! The pond monster has got me! He won't let me go!"

Quickly, Freddie grabbed Chipper's hand. Darla grabbed the other, and they tried to pull their friend from the terrifying clutches of the pond monster.

"He won't let go!" Chipper shouted again. "He's got me! He's really got me!"

"Pull harder, Darla!" Freddie shouted.

Finally, Chipper's foot was free, and the three first graders tumbled backward, falling into the tall grass. Mr. Chewy leapt out of the way, or they would have landed on top of him!

"That was close!" Chipper said, heaving a sigh of relief. "The pond monster had my foot, and he wouldn't let go!"

Freddie looked at Chipper's sneaker. It was covered with thick, black, gooey muck.

"Wait a minute," he said, pointing at Chipper's foot. "You weren't attacked by the pond monster. Your foot was stuck in the mud, that's all."

Chipper looked at his dirty shoe. "Well, it sure *felt* like I was being attacked by the pond monster."

The three first graders scrambled to their feet. Chipper found a stick and scraped the black muck from his shoe.

"It's still dirty and wet," Darla said.

Chipper shrugged. "It'll dry," he said.

"Come on," Freddie said. "Let's keep looking for the pond monster." He pointed to the ground. "The tracks lead this way."

He started walking. Chipper followed, then Darla, and Mr. Chewy. Freddie kept careful watch on the ground, following the tracks as they wound through the tall grass and plants. On the other side of the pond, the tracks veered into the woods.

The three first graders stopped and stared into the forest.

"Maybe the pond monster is hiding in the woods," Chipper said.

"Maybe he's watching us right now," Darla said.

They remained quiet for a few moments,

their eyes searching around trees and branches, looking for any sign of the pond monster.

"Let's keep following the tracks," Freddie said. "I'm sure they'll lead us to the pond monster."

"That's what I'm afraid of," Darla said. "Maybe we should just go home and play a game."

"We'll be all right," Freddie said. "If we see the pond monster, we'll stay away from him."

"But Freddie," Darla said, "what if he doesn't want to stay away from us? What if he wants to have us for lunch?"

"Maybe he doesn't eat people," said Chipper. "Let's go, Freddie. Come on, Darla."

Freddie started walking again, following the tracks into the forest. Chipper and Darla were behind him, and Mr. Chewy followed.

But it wasn't long before they stopped again, because the tracks they had been following stopped in front of a large, thick bush.

"The tracks lead right into this bush," Freddie whispered. *"He might be watching us at this very moment."*

The three first graders stared into the bush . . . and it didn't take long before they saw the giant, dark eyes staring back at them . . . .

11

Freddie, Chipper, and Darla froze. They could see the pair of eyes, glaring back at them from within the bush.

"It's him!" Chipper hissed. *"It's the pond monster! He's in the bushes!"*

They continued staring through the branches. Because there were so many leaves, they couldn't see the pond monster clearly. The only thing they could see were his eyes, staring back at them from within the bushes.

"I told you," Darla whispered. "I told you this wasn't a good idea. Now, we're going to get gobbled up. We're going to get gobbled up, and my mom and dad are going to be really mad."

Chipper rolled his eyes and spoke. spoke. "Darla," he began, "if you get gobbled up, what will it matter if your mom and dad get mad? They can't send you to your room and give you a time out if you've been gobbled up."

Darla had to think about this for a moment. "Still," she said, "they're going to be mad. I knew we shouldn't have followed the tracks into the woods!"

"Okay," Freddie said, "here's what we do. Let's move back. Go really slow. We don't want to do anything to make the pond monster mad."

The three first graders backed up very slowly. Branches and twigs snapped beneath their shoes. Mr. Chewy, too, moved cautiously. He was just as scared as the three first graders.

The bush trembled, ever so slightly. A branch moved. Leaves flickered.

Suddenly, branches parted, and the pond monster lunged at the three first graders!

12

Freddie spun around and started to run, but he ran into Chipper. Both fell, knocking Darla down, too. The three tumbled to the ground, and Mr. Chewy had to dart out of the way to keep from getting squished.

Luckily for the three first graders, the creature that emerged from the bushes wasn't the pond monster . . . it was only Mr. and Mrs. Beaker's dog, Booper!

The big dog trotted up to Freddie and began licking his face.

"Booper!" Freddie said. He patted the dog's head and scratched his ears. "Boy, am I glad it's you, and not the pond monster!"

Mr. Chewy hid behind Freddie's leg, hoping that the large dog wouldn't see him. After all: he was a cat, and many dogs chase cats.

Booper, however, didn't see Mr. Chewy. The dog barked once, wagged his tail, and ran off.

Freddie, Chipper, and Darla got to their feet and brushed themselves off.

"Booper really scared me," Darla said.

"Me, too," Chipper said with a laugh. He pointed to the ground. "And look . . . the tracks we were following aren't from the pond monster. They were made by Booper."

Freddie put his hands on his hips. "And so far, we haven't been able to find the pond monster," he said.

"I'll bet he's in the pond," Darla said. "I'll bet he's hiding in the water, waiting for us to get close. Then, he's going to gobble us up."

On the other side of the pond, the fisherman still stood on the dock, holding his fishing pole. The clouds had gone away, and the sun was shining. The blue sky could be seen on the surface of the pond.

Suddenly, the man's fishing pole bent over. The man held the rod tightly. In the middle of the pond, the water boiled and churned.

"I've got him!" the man exclaimed. "I've got the monster on the line! I hope he doesn't get away this time!"

Oh, the creature wasn't going to get away.

Not this time.

Freddie, Chipper, and Darla were just minutes from finding out the truth about the pond monster.

13

"Come on!" Freddie shouted. "Let's go watch the fisherman catch the pond monster!"

The three first graders and Mr. Chewy ran along the shore of the pond, but they stopped when they reached the dock.

"It's a monster, all right!" the man shouted as he battled the creature.

"Is he going to bite you?" Darla shouted.

"Well," the man said as he continued to

reel in the monster, "he's got very sharp teeth. I'll have to be careful."

This frightened the three first graders.

"Maybe we should get out of here," Chipper said. "I don't want to get bitten by the pond monster."

"Yeah," Darla said. "The fisherman is probably making the monster really, really mad. What if he comes after us?"

"Let's ask the fisherman," Freddie said.

"Hey," he called out, "if we come out on the dock, will that thing hurt us?"

The fisherman was still holding his fishing pole and reeling the monster in. He shook his head.

"I don't think so," he said, "but when I get him in the net, you'll want to keep away from his mouth."

Freddie, Chipper, and Darla cautiously

made their way out onto the dock. They watched the man as he gripped his fishing pole, which was bent over from the strong pull of the pond monster.

Suddenly, disaster struck. The man had been standing near the edge of the dock, and without warning, he lost his footing . . . and fell into the water.

The monster had pulled him into the pond!

14

There was a huge splash as the man landed in the water. Freddie, Chipper, and Darla gasped.

"He's going to be eaten by the pond monster!" Darla shouted. "He pulled him in, and now he's going to gobble him up!"

Thankfully, the water wasn't very deep, and the man was able to stand up. Water came up over his waist, and he was soaking wet, but he still had a tight grip on his fishing pole.

"Are you all right?" Freddie asked.

"I'm fine," the man said. "Lucky for me, I didn't drop my fishing pole. I don't want this one to get away."

The fisherman continued to battle with the pond monster. He held his fishing pole tightly and continued to reel in the line. Water splashed as he pulled the pond monster closer and closer.

"I can't bear to watch!" Darla said, and she covered her eyes with her hands.

The fisherman stopped reeling in the line. With one hand, he held the fishing pole, and with the other, he snatched the net from the dock. He held the pole high in the air, dipped the net into the water, made a sudden sweep . . . and caught the pond monster!

"Wait a minute!" Freddie said, after he saw the huge creature in the net. "That's not a monster at all!"

And it wasn't! Captured in the net was a very large, long, dark-colored fish with gray spots and a white belly.

Darla pulled her hands away from her eyes. "What is *that?!?!*" she asked.

"It's some sort of fish!" Chipper said. "And it's huge!"

"It's a northern pike!" the man said. He held up the net, and the three first graders leaned in for a closer look. The fish flopped around and tried to get out of the net, but it couldn't.

The man, still standing in the water and dripping wet, waded closer to the dock to give Freddie, Chipper, and Darla a better look at the fish.

"That thing is almost as big as me!" Freddie said.

The man nodded. "A northern pike can grow very big," he said, "sometimes, up to fifty inches long. This one is a monster."

Darla spoke. "So, he's a fish and not a real monster?"

The man shook his head. "What I mean is that the fish is very big. Sometimes, a big fish is called a 'monster' because of its size."

"Oh, I get it," Chipper said. "So, there really is no pond monster?"

The man shook his head. "Just this one," the man said.

"But we threw a stuffed bunny rabbit into the pond, and it was eaten," Darla said.

"I'm not surprised," the man replied. "Northern pike will eat just about anything. To him, the stuffed rabbit probably looked like food."

While Freddie, Chipper, and Darla

watched, the man placed his fishing pole on the dock. Then, he placed the net containing the fish on the dock. With both hands, he carefully removed the hook from the fish's mouth.

"You have to be very careful with these fish," he said. "They have very sharp teeth."

It was true. When the pike opened its mouth, rows and rows of very sharp teeth could be seen.

After the man had removed the hook, he picked up the giant fish and held it carefully in his arms. Then, he gently lowered it to the water and let it go. With a giant splash, the huge fish was gone.

"There," the man said. "Now, he'll grow even bigger, and maybe one of you young folks can catch him someday."

"Wow," Freddie said. "I can't imagine

catching a fish that big! He would probably pull me into the water, too!"

The man climbed onto the dock and stood. Water dripped from his sopped clothing. "Well," he said, "I guess I'd better get home and get out of these wet clothes." He picked up his fishing pole, net, and tackle box. "You kids have fun today," he said as he walked away.

"We will," Freddie called out. "We always have a lot of fun."

"So, there really is no such thing as a pond monster," Darla said as they watched the fisherman walk away. "I guess my brother was only fooling us."

"That's all right," Chipper said. "We learned what a northern pike is, and got to see one up close."

"Yeah," Freddie said. "In a way, it was

sort of a monster. It just wasn't the kind of monster we were expecting."

"I have an idea," Chipper said. "Now that our hunt for the pond monster is over, let's see if we can find that bullfrog. He was a monster, too!"

"That sounds like fun," Freddie said. "Maybe if the three of us work together, we might be able to catch him!"

"I'm not touching any frog," Darla said. "Frogs are icky."

"Frogs aren't icky," Freddie said. "Frogs are cool."

"But you can help us look," Chipper said.

"Okay," said Darla, "but there is no way I'm going to touch one."

But the three first graders weren't going to find the bullfrog.

Instead, they would find something else in the water . . . something that would to yet another zany, crazy adventure!

NEXT:
FREDDIE FERNORTNER,
FEARLESS FIRST GRADER
BOOK ELEVEN:

TADPOLE TROUBLE!

CONTINUE ON TO READ
THE FIRST CHAPTER FOR
FREE!

1

Freddie Fernortner, fearless first grader, was excited. So was Chipper, one of his best friends.

But Darla—another one of Freddie's best friends—wasn't excited.

You see, the three friends had decided to look for frogs at a nearby pond. Freddie and Chipper wanted to catch one, but Darla didn't. She didn't like frogs.

"I think all frogs are icky," she told Freddie and Chipper.

"Frogs are not icky," Chipper said. "They're cool."

"Yeah," Freddie said. "It would be fun to catch one."

"I'm not touching any frog," Darla said, shaking her head. "I'll help you look, but I'm not going to get close."

Together, they walked the short distance to the pond. Freddie's cat, Mr. Chewy, followed, happily chewing his gum and blowing bubbles.

The pond wasn't very big. It was surrounded by bushes and cattails. There was a long dock that went out over the water.

The sun was shining, and the sky was blue. A few birds chirped, and a light wind caused the cattails on the other side of the pond to sway gently.

Freddie pointed. "Let's look over there," he said, "on the other side of the pond."

"I can't wait to catch a frog!" said Chipper. "I caught one last summer, at the park."

"I hope he doesn't bite you," Darla said.

"Frogs don't bite!" Chipper and Freddie both said at the same time.

"My brother says frogs have big teeth," Darla said.

"Your brother is just fooling you," said Chipper. "He just wants—"

Suddenly, Freddie pointed into the water and shouted. "Look!" he cried. "Look at that!"

Chipper and Darla looked at where Freddie was pointing, and the three first graders were amazed at what they were seeing.

WATCH FOR MORE *FREDDIE FERNORTNER, FEARLESS FIRST GRADER* BOOKS, COMING SOON!